I0689442

SET TO YOUR FREQUENCY

Poems From the Last First Love
By Vanessa Stevens

ISBN: 979-8-9995594-0-1 (Paperback)

To SKB,

Three weeks changed everything—

and somehow, so did the days that followed.

You opened my heart, filled my soul,

and showed me that love—real love—

can bloom again, no matter when it finds us.

Our story is still writing itself,

growing slowly, tenderly, truthfully.

And no matter what the outcome,

this love, our love,

will always live in me

as memory, as lesson,

as one of the most beautiful truths

I've ever known.

Author's Note

These poems are written in the voice of Vanessa Stevens—a woman in her fifties, seasoned by life, scarred by love, and yet still brave enough to try again.

She is sensual, soulful, strong—but learning to be soft again.

She is healing. She is learning. She is remembering what it means to be loved and seen.

Through heartbreak, passion, and rediscovery, Vanessa shares what it feels like to fall—fast, deep, and without a safety net. These poems are her journey through the highs, the hurt, the silence, and the return.

This is not a fairytale.

This is a woman's truth.

Told in rhythm.

Told in reflection.

Told in love.

"Love after fifty is not late, it's layered. It knows loss, carries wisdom, and still dares to hope."

Table of Contents

Part 1: The Spark & The Rush

Vanessa didn't fall in love. She dove.

After years of guarded independence, this love burst through like sunlight after rain.

What began as curiosity became connection... then chemistry... then soul-deep surrender.

She wasn't just seen. She was met. And then, she was touched in a way that rewired her.

"Some loves are soft from the start. Ours was a flame that whispered, 'You're home.'"

The Fear, The Fall, The Love

It started with a match. Two hearts aligned.

A flicker in the dark that became wildfire by morning.

By sunrise, my soul already recognized yours.

By mid-morning, you were speaking forever like we had always

known.

Breakfast never happened.

Lunch turned into something holy.

The way your eyes held mine

said more than words ever could.

You looked at me like you already knew

what I hadn't yet admitted.

You broke me wide open with that Brooklyn calm.

That soldier stillness.

Those hands didn't just touch. They told truth.

Every hour with you unfolded a softer version of me.

By night seven, we were wrapped in rhythm.

By night seven, I knew.

Week two. We spoke of homes.

Of plans.

Of life beyond the now.

Fear crept in wearing the face of logic.

I second-guessed paradise.

I overthought joy.

I chose control instead of connection.

If I could go back,

I would whisper grace into that woman's ear.

I would tell her she didn't have to be scared when it felt right.

You held my soul in your hands, and I flinched.

You kissed my wounds, and I pulled away.

But I see you still.

In every morning light.

In every quiet thought.

Let's rewrite this.

Let's rebuild.

What we had was never just a spark.

It was a flame with our names on it.

Three Weeks of Forever

Fun fact.

You made me laugh with the kind of joy that felt like freedom.

Day and night, I floated through our time

as if I had been waiting my whole life

for someone to talk to me the way you did.

Three weeks.

That's all it took to rearrange my stars.

My friends saw it. The glow. The ease.

Even strangers felt the warmth I carried

in my cheeks, my walk, my voice.

We didn't need TV.

No music. No distractions.

Just your voice.

A melody I didn't know I needed.

"Let's explore that," you would say,

turning casual conversations into constellations.

I still trace them in my memory.

You made curiosity feel sexy.

You made silence feel like a gift.

And yes, three weeks may sound like a blink.

But with you, time expanded.

We built something infinite inside borrowed days.

A universe of laughter, gentle discovery, soul-naked honesty.

Three weeks of forever.

A love that was brief

but etched on my bones.

Drunk on Your Lips

Our first kiss wasn't just a kiss.

It was awakening, soft, slow, and potent enough

to ruin every kiss that came before it.

Drunk on your lips, I whispered "loft sips" in my head.

Like a prayer. Like a spell. I couldn't explain it.

Your lips?

They weren't just soft.

They knew. They spoke.

They claimed me. Gently. Completely.

You said mine were soft too.

Like a confession you didn't mean to say out loud.

And in that moment, I bloomed.

You opened doors.

Not just the chivalrous kind.

You opened emotional gateways.

You made me feel feminine without making me feel small.

You led without pushing.

You guided without control.

Alpha. Omega. Everything in between.

With you, I wasn't afraid to follow.

"Loft sips," I would whisper in the dark,
aching to taste you again.

That kiss didn't just spark lust.
It whispered of destiny.
It made me believe in beginnings.
In belonging.
In a mouth that could make a woman remember
what it means to be seen.

When Two Worlds Meet

You're Brooklyn-born, Southern-bred.

Grit in your voice. Gentle in your touch.

A streetwise gentleman with steel in your spine and a slow drawl

that lingers.

You say what you mean.

You mean what you say.

No trial version. No charm on a timer.

You are consistent. With me. With the world.

A man of foundation.

More than roots — you are an anchor.

More than muscle — you carry meaning.

I'm spoken word with Southern roots.

Fire wrapped in softness. A storm that rhymes before it roars.

I write to feel. You build to protect.

I fall in metaphors. You rise in movement.

We shouldn't work.

Not on paper. Not in theory.

But the way you see me

and the way I settle in your presence

rewrites all of that.

You don't flinch at my overthinking.

I don't run from your silence.

We're learning how to dance.

You move with steady steps.

I move with wild sway.

We don't talk the same, but you hear me.

We don't love the same, but I feel you.

You lead with action.

I follow with trust.

You stay grounded.

I rise in you.

We're not opposites.

We're aligned.

Two roots.

One rhythm.

You are Georgia soil and Brooklyn brick.

I am cotton fields and city streets.

And still, somehow, this feels like home.

Not a house. Not a place.

But you.

A compass. A stillness.

Two worlds that didn't need to change

just learn how to belong.

It Was You

I never asked for this.
Not again. Not now.

I had made peace with being solo.
Learned to dance alone.
Slept in the middle of the bed,
convinced myself I was full.

But then, you.
With a calm I didn't recognize
and a patience that didn't scare me.

You didn't come to fix me.
You came to know me.

You didn't ask for more than I could give,
but still made me want to give more.

You listened.
Not to respond, but to understand.
And in your stillness, I found breath.

I used to dream of being chosen.
But you made me feel claimed.
Not owned. Seen.

You made soft feel safe again.

You showed me that love could be quiet.

Uncomplicated. Still.

You touched the places

I had kept wrapped in silence.

Not with pressure. With presence.

It wasn't a grand gesture.

It wasn't a confession.

It was how you looked at me

when I wasn't trying.

If peace had a name,

it would be yours.

I didn't go looking.

But now that you're here,

I know it was always you.

Because of you,

I reach without fear.

I rest without apology.

I speak without shrinking.

And for the first time in years,

I believe in forever again.

Who Loved First?

It was a quiet knowing.

Not something said.

Something felt.

In glances.

In pauses.

In the way we lingered a little longer than necessary.

We never said the words.

Not then.

But love lived in the way you watched me sleep.

In the way I memorized your voice.

In how we let silence fill the room without fear.

You joked about it.

Said one day you'd claim I said it first.

Maybe I did.

Not with words,

but in the way my body melted into yours.

In how my voice softened

when you walked in the room.

You listened when I told you my secrets.

Not just the stories.

The shame.

The kind of truth I hadn't spoken in years.

And you didn't flinch.

You held it like something sacred.

That night,

when you pulled me close

and whispered something silly just to make me laugh,

my heart screamed the words

my lips were too afraid to say.

So, who loved first?

Does it matter?

We both felt it.

We both knew.

And even if we never say it the same way,

my body already answered you.

Skin to Skin

It was that night.

The one we both knew was coming.

We pressed play on a movie,

but neither of us saw a thing.

The tension lived in the silence between us.

Not awkward. Not rushed. Just waiting.

A kiss.

Slow.

Deliberate.

One that didn't ask for permission.

It offered it.

Tongue met tongue.

Fingertips mapped skin.

We moved like we already knew the steps.

Clothes fell to the floor like promises kept.

You peeled me open with nothing but your palms.

Skin to skin.

Breath to breath.

Your body aligned with mine

like it had been made to fit me.

And when you entered me,
my name still warm in your mouth,
it wasn't just sex.
It was surrender.

You read my body like scripture.
Paused in places no one ever stayed long enough to learn.

Each stroke, a prayer.
Each gasp, a vow.

You took your time.
Not to tease. To treasure.

After, you held me like I was worth keeping.

No rush.
No words.
Just stillness.

Sweat cooling where heat once claimed us.
Fingers tangled. Legs still touching.

Skin to skin.
And a silence that said more
than love ever could.

Part 2: The Break & The Silence

Just when the love felt destined, fear crept in.

Misunderstandings bloomed in silence.

Vulnerability turned to retreat.

Vanessa's overthinking collided with his emotional shutdown.

There were no goodbyes.

Only space. Distance. Quiet ache.

"Grief has its own language—mine still speaks your name."

The Silence Between Us

It didn't end with shouting.

Just silence.

A pause that turned into distance.

A breath that never came back.

You shut down.

I spiraled.

And the space between us

grew louder than any argument.

No explanation.

No fight.

Just gone.

You knew my fear.

You knew I was still learning to open.

But you let silence answer

what I never dared to ask.

There were no slammed doors.

No unread texts.

Just your quiet retreat,

measured and controlled.

I filled the silence with questions.

Tried to read between pauses.

Wrote stories in my head

to explain the one you never told.

And now, weeks later,

you still echo

in everything I try to move past.

Not the pain of goodbye.

The ache of never getting one.

My smile is still cracked.

My bed is still too big.

I keep checking for closure

like mail that won't come.

Even your ghost is consistent.

Even your absence knows how to stay.

Shadows of Trust

Could we find our way back?

Should I dare to trust?

The fear of betrayal turns love to dust.

You cut me deep.

Broke me in two.

Now every shadow reminds me of you.

Three weeks gone, yet the ache remains.

Memories etched like unyielding stains.

We shared our lives,

our hearts, our dreams.

Now I'm left with unanswered screams.

I want to date, to move ahead,

but thoughts of you echo instead.

Will I compare each voice, each face

to the love we built in such brief embrace?

You were my anchor,my daily call.
Now silence looms,

a deafening wall.
How could God let this pain unfold?
A love so warm, now bitter cold.

Should I scream,

or should I pray
for healing, for light,

to find my way?
But trust feels distant, out of reach—
a lesson learned that love can teach.

Could we find our way back?

Should I try?
Or is this love meant only to die?
A part of me hopes.

A part of me fears,
caught between longing and unshed tears.

The Hurt That Lingers

You said I didn't do anything wrong,

but then you left.

No words.

No warning.

Just silence loud enough to bruise my heart.

I replay our last conversation

the laughter, the warmth,

the way you said "talk soon."

But soon never came.

You disappeared like a ghost,

and I was left haunted.

Not just by your absence,

but by the possibility that I misread it all.

How could something so real go unreal that fast?

How could a man so steady become so still?

I questioned everything.

Was I too much?

Too open?

Too fast with my feelings?

Too slow with my fear?

I didn't just lose you.

I lost the rhythm we were building,

the breath between our words,

the quiet safety of us.

People say let it go.

Move on.

But where do you place love that had no funeral?

No ending. Just absence.

This is the hurt that lingers.

Not the pain of goodbye.

The ache of *never getting one.*

Part 3: The Ache of Absence

She missed him in the moments that mattered.

Small victories, favorite songs, bedtime routines.

Vanessa didn't just grieve the man. She grieved the future, the rhythm, the hope.

She tried to forget him. She couldn't.

And the truth began to emerge it wasn't just him who left, her fear helped push him out.

"Heartbreak doesn't end love. It reveals what was real."

Five Weeks Later

I miss you terribly,

in ways words cannot hold.

Silence weighs heavy,

where conversations

once unfolded.

Peaky Blinders pulls me in,

and I ache to share it with you.

Your house says "pending"—

a milestone I wish I could applaud too.

I miss our daily check-ins,

morning, moon, and night.

The way we shared our worlds

made everything feel right.

I finished PMP Bootcamp

and long to tell you it's done.

To share the hurdles crossed.

To hear your pride, your voice, your smile.

And still, you haunt me.
Not as a villain, but as a ghost.

I missed your voice in my morning quiet.
Missed your "did you eat?"
and the ease of existing beside someone
who asked for nothing but presence.

Now I understand.
Not all endings are loud.
Some unravel in whispers.
Some goodbyes don't come with closure—
just quiet.

And quiet is its own kind of wound.

What the Music Knew

Every song carries your name.

A voice from the speakers ignites the flame.

The opening notes hit—

and I'm undone.

I want to sing what's already in my chest,

but I can't.

Because you're not here.

Love didn't fade with the music.

It fused into every note.

You left the room,

but the melody stayed.

Now every chorus

feels like a memory

trying to sing me back to you.

At nine,

I sang heartbreak like I understood it.

A child with no reason to cry... yet.

But now, I do.

Now I know

why Adele breaks.

Why Toni pleads.

Why Jazmine burns.

The love songs of my life

used to be background noise.

Now they are mirrors.

Now they are scripture.

I don't just hear music anymore.

I feel it.

I live inside it.

I bleed inside it.

And when no one's watching,

I cry together with the girl

who didn't yet know

how much a chorus could hurt.

The Stages of You

When will the pain end?

When will it subside?

This grief feels endless,

like a wave I can't outride.

Were you really the one,

or am I chasing shadows?

A hopeless romantic,

yearning for what I'll never know.

The stages of grief move slow.

Denial whispered, "It's a mistake."

Depression weighed on everything I touched.

Bargaining kept me up at night.

I begged God to rewind us.

To let one of us bend before we broke.

I waited for anger to set me free,

but I couldn't hate you.

Not even then. Not even now.

Acceptance still feels like a stranger

distant, polite,

but never quite at home in my chest.

You're not just a memory.

You're a question.

A ghost that knocks

whenever old love songs play.

I keep looking for closure

in places you no longer live.

And maybe that's the cruelest part

realizing grief doesn't ask for permission.

It just moves in.

But I'm learning now

that grief doesn't mean I'm stuck.

It means I loved deep enough to be altered.

And slowly, softly,

I'm starting to forgive

the story we didn't get to finish.

What Fear Stole

Anxiety whispered
where love should have been,
planting doubts deep within.

If you didn't call,

my heart would race.
I worried someone else had taken my place.

I didn't know what it was back then
just that fear would twist, would bend.

Overthinking, assumptions, an unspoken fight.
I pushed you away in the dead of night.

My darkest secret didn't break you in two.
But my spiraling thoughts became the glue
that held me back from loving whole.
My anxiety was a thief of soul.

I walked away,

shut down in fear.

But losing you?

I couldn't bear.

You couldn't hang

and who could blame you?

My fears consumed

what we tried to claim.

Now I see it clearer,

but it's too late to change the start.

I handed fear the keys

and watched it drive you from my heart.

Love didn't fail.
I did.

Because fear always asks the wrong questions

and never waits for love to answer.

No One But You

I wandered through faces,
rushed past voices,
chased echoes of something

I once held close.

They were charming.
They were clever.
They smiled just right
but they weren't you.

Conversations turned hollow.
Laughter rang thin.
No fire sparked.
No gravity pulled.

I measured them in shadows,
in the weight of your name,
in the way my heart stayed still
when it once used to race.

What am I to do

when the world is full of almost,

but my soul still aches for only you?

I tried.

I showed up.

I smiled when I didn't feel like it.

But no hand felt like home.

You are the blueprint.

The sound in the silence.

The ache I can't rewrite.

And though I move forward,

bit by bit,

my spirit still turns toward the echo of us.

Part 4: The Rekindling

Healing didn't come with flowers. It came with a text. Then a call. Then a moment.

Vanessa didn't rush back, she listened.

She softened. So did he.

The love returned, not as fire, but as warmth, curiosity, and choice.

They began again; not from scratch, but from truth.

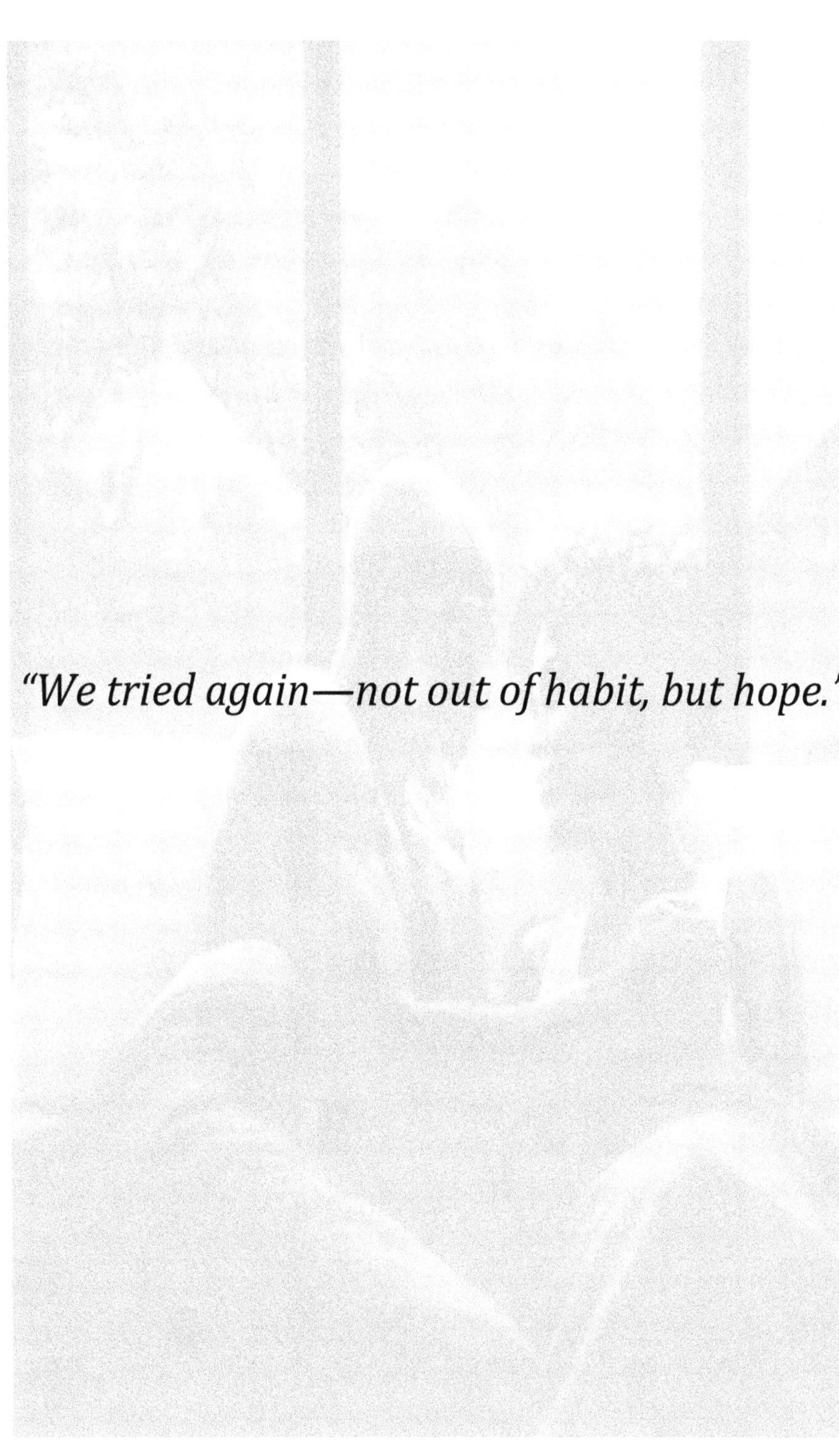

"We tried again—not out of habit, but hope."

Slow and Steady

A quick hello.

A simple reply.

Still, it sent a tremor through my guarded heart.

I didn't think you would…

but you did.

You reached for me

like time had never skipped a beat.

Then another check-in,

and I couldn't hide my glee

smiling at my screen,

afraid to believe in second chances.

Day three, your voice filled the line.

You'd closed on your home,

and somehow, you wanted me to know.

Is this the beginning?

Can we start anew?

Or is this just a moment;

a flicker in the dark?

Okay.

Let's slow down.

Let's take our time.

Let's tread softly on the bridge

between past and possibility.

I'm not rushing in.

You're not dragging me forward.

But the rhythm feels familiar.

The trust?

It's starting to hum again.

Maybe this time,

we will build something that lasts.

Love Not Lost

Let the healing begin.

Soft and slow.

Like the first rays of dawn

breaking through the night.

We share our lives again

morning whispers,

evening check-ins,

a rhythm both familiar and new.

Could this be a new beginning?

Love not lost, just paused

a story waiting for its next chapter to unfold.

But let's slow down.

Tread gently.

Wounds once torn

must be stitched with care.

It's time to talk

the silence,

the breaking,

the moment we splintered apart.

Can we piece it back together?

The words come light but direct.

Misunderstanding clears

like the sky after rain.

My heart races,

pounding against my ribs.

Could this be real?

Could this be us again?

Not a fantasy.

Not a rebound.

But a love

resurrected by truth.

Building Us Again

Now that the air is clear,

we start again.

Back to fun facts

and let's explore.

Back to laughter

wrapped in knowing glances.

Picking out furniture.

Discussing paint and fixtures.

Not quite a move-in,

but a whispered promise in the making.

The love never left.

It simply waited.

Patient. Steady. Unshaken.

Rooted in respect.

Wrapped in admiration.

I can't stop smiling,

lost in the warmth of your touch,

the press of your lips—

so familiar, so right.

We are finding our way.

Brick by brick.

Moment by moment.

There's no rush.

No blueprint.

Just a deep knowing

that what we're building this time

has a stronger foundation.

Not a return.

A rebuild.

A better version of *us.*

New Yet Familiar

The first time,

we stumbled over silence.

Words tangled in fear,

not of love, but of space.

Of what it meant to share the night.

Not bodies, but breaths.

Not passion, but presence.

Would I fit beside you?

Would you rest beside me?

We cleared the air,

but the question lingered.

And now, six months later,

you ask me to stay.

Just for a night.

Just to see.

A little touch and go.

Hesitant hands.

Shifting weight.

Learning the rhythm of closeness
all over again.

But then, the magic settles in.

Our heartbeats find the same tempo.

The night folds us gently into each other.

I wake to sunlight spilling gold over your skin—
bright, blinding, beautiful.

And I know now:

you are my peace.

And I am your light.

New.

Yet familiar.

Whole.

Part 5: This Time With Grace

Love doesn't always roar when it returns.

Sometimes it walks in slowly; barefoot, familiar,

with nothing to prove but everything to give.

This is the part where we've learned each other.

Where laughter returns like sunlight,

and desire deepens with knowing.

It's where we say "I see you," not through fantasy,

but through the daily rhythm of real love.

This time, we don't rush.

We just stay.

"This time, I choose me first—and still leave room for us."

Smile

You make me smile.

Not just sometimes,

but in the middle of the ordinary.

At work, I smile.

Driving, I smile.

At the gym,

I catch myself grinning,

thinking of something you said,

something you did,

or just the way you see me.

It's not a performance smile.

It's not for anyone else.

It starts in my chest

and curls up to my lips

before I even notice.

You make me feel good.

Not just loved, alive.

I love our pillow talk

after a long, beautiful session of love,

or even when it's fast and satisfying.

You always take the time to bask in the afterglow.

You hold me, breathe with me, laugh with me.

And I open up in ways

I never have before.

You talk.

You listen.

Listen, listen...

I didn't even know how much I needed

someone to hear me

just so I could finally hear myself.

And now, I smile.

Because it's real.

Because it's you.

Because you feel like peace.

Already Yours

I haven't said the words.

Not yet.

Not out loud.

But my body already told you.

My eyes too.

The way I lean into your hand.

The way I pause when you speak.

How your voice calms the spin in my mind.

I want to say, "I love you."

Want to scream it.

Write it across the sky.

Post it, tag it, let the world know

"I got a man."

And not just any man. You.

But that's not your way.

You don't need labels or declarations.

You just need real.

You ask, "Don't I show up for you in every way?"

And you do.

Quietly.

Consistently.

Wholly.

You care for my children like they were yours.

You protect my peace without asking for applause.

And that made me see; I don't need the world to know.

Because you know.

And I feel it.

In every touch.

Every call.

Every "You good, baby?"

when I didn't even realize I wasn't.

So maybe I'll wait to say those three words,

but truth is….

I already love you.

I already feel yours.

I don't need to share you

to know you're already mine.

Set To Your Frequency

Your voice makes me vibrate.
The timber of your words—
how do you make simple things
like Fun Fact

or let's explore that
melt right through me?

Maybe you've said them before,
but from now on,
they'll touch me in places no one else can.

You asked me why I react like I do.
I didn't have the words. Only the ache.
It's like one touch from you
and I'm set on fire.

I ache for you.
I can't control my body.

My fluids soak me to the core.

And all I want is more. And more.

The first time, I thought I couldn't take you all.

But now, I can't get enough.

The vibrations between us

are like nothing I've ever known.

You set me aflame.

You keep me wet.

You ask,

"Why me?"

Why only you?

And I don't know how to explain it.

Except that every nerve I have

waits for your name

to be spoken in my ear.

Because of You

You told me,
"This is a two-way street."

And I heard you.
Not just the words,
but the want.

You asked me to show up.
To lean in.
To reach for you.
Not just to receive,
but to invite.

So here I am.
In boy shorts.
In high heels.
Moving with music meant just for you.
Dancing like you're the only one watching
because you are.

I'm shy.

Always have been.

No one's ever asked me

to be bold in this way.

But I want to please you.

Not because you demand it,

but because you wait.

Because you ache.

Because you let me know

you want to be wanted too.

So tonight,

I'll tease.

I'll whisper.

I'll pull you closer with every glance.

No hesitation.

No doubt.

I'm not just on the street.

I'm walking it—

because of you.

That Man

You fixed a vacuum like it was nothing,
then repaired a busted window on a car
that wasn't even yours.

You hung drywall like art,
sealed cracks like you were sealing time.
You could build a whole damn house
with your bare hands.
And I believe you have.

I've never known a man who could move like that.
Confident. Steady.
Making hard things look easy.

No applause needed.
No bragging.
Just done.

You don't talk about it.
You live it.

And that kind of quiet power?
It's sexy as hell.

I used to call you my Superman,
but that felt too simple.

You're not fantasy. You're real.

A man who knows his tools,
his timing, his worth.

You show up.
You solve.
You handle it.

And when you touch me
after all that strength
it's like finding softness
where I never expected it.

I watch you work, and I melt.
Because it's not just what you fix.
It's how you move.
How you carry the knowing,
like it was born in you.

No flex. No front.
Just power.
Just calm.
Just... that man I get to want.

Becoming Her

I'm learning how to be your woman.

Not by losing myself,

but by becoming more of me.

You don't mold me.

You mirror back the best version

I forgot I could be.

You push me

not for you, but for me.

And for my children.

Somehow,

that makes me want to rise for you too.

You show me what pleases you.

What not to do.

How to hold you.

When to let go.

You lead, but never dominate.

You guide, without control.

It's in the way you speak.

The way you correct me.

The way you offer space

but hold me close.

I didn't know love could teach like this.

Not loud.

Not cruel.

Not demanding.

But gentle.

Direct.

Intentional.

You're not trying to change me.

You just ask me to try.

And baby, I do.

Because when I see the way you look at me

not just in lust,

but in belief

I want to grow

into the woman who already lives in your eyes.

Acts of Service

Your heart moves without audience.

Not just for me,

but for anyone lucky enough to cross your path.

You don't perform love.

You practice it.

With hands that build,

feet that show up,

and time that adjusts without being asked.

You told me your love language was acts of service—

and then lived it daily.

No praise. No points.

Just presence.

You help.

You fix.

Even your silence feels like support.

Are you perfect? No.

But you are present.

And that feels like grace.

You take my words seriously.
You hold space when I fall apart.

When I said I loved full beards,
you grew one—itch and all.
When I said I needed more calls,
you didn't just dial.
You showed up.

That's not charm.
That's care.

The kind that settles a woman's nervous system.
The kind that says "I'm falling for you"
without needing to say a word.

And yes, my heart hears it.
Every time you show up,
I feel it falling for you too.

Love Letter To Us

Dear Sister,

This book was born in heartbreak, but it finishes in hope.

If you're holding these pages, maybe you've known the ache of disappointment. Maybe you've been lied to, walked out on, ignored, or mishandled. Maybe you've spent years being strong; not because you wanted to be, but because no one ever gave you room not to be.

This is for you.

For the woman who thought love was for everyone else. For the woman who got divorced after decades and wondered if there was anything left of herself beneath all the titles, routines, and survival. For the woman over 50 who didn't think her knees would ever buckle again, not from pain, but from love. For the woman who couldn't imagine submitting. Not because she didn't want to, but because she had never met a man who was worthy of her surrender.

Let me be clear. This isn't about submission the way the world defines it. It's not about control or erasing yourself to boost someone else's ego. I'm talking about choosing softness because you've finally been given a reason to rest. Because he leads without force. Because he sees you fully. Because with him, you don't have to shrink or chase or prove.

You may have to kiss a few frogs. You may have to heal first. You may have to sit with yourself long enough to stop romanticizing chaos and start recognizing peace.

But please, don't water yourself down. Don't settle for the "perfect couple" on social media. Don't accept a highlight reel when your soul is craving a safe place to land.

And please, don't resign yourself to loneliness just because you're not twenty-five anymore. Real love doesn't have an expiration date. The kind of love that makes you feel safe, held, seen, and still entirely yourself exists. And when it finds you, you'll know. You won't have to chase it. You won't have to beg for it. You won't have to guess.

It will feel like home.

So, stay open. Stay whole. Stay rooted in who you are. Don't harden. Don't close off. Don't become so self-sufficient that you forget you still deserve softness. There is someone out there who is meant for you and only you. You don't have to be perfect. You just have to be ready.

For love that finally feels like home.

With love,
Vanessa